POEMS THAT SING TO YOU

POEMS THAT

Illustrations by Alan Leiner

SING TO YOU

Selected by Michael R. Strickland

WORDSONG
Boyds Mills Press

For my parents, Dorothy Salley
and Maurice Raymond Strickland—M.R.S.

To Ilsa, the love of my life—A.L.

Text copyright © 1993 by Michael R. Strickland
Illustrations copyright © 1993 by Boyds Mills Press

Published by Wordsong
Boyds Mills Press, Inc.
A Highlights Company
815 Church Street
Honesdale, PA 18431
Printed in Mexico

Publisher Cataloging-in-Publication Data
Main entry under title.
    Poems that sing to you / selected by Michael R. Strickland ; illustrations by
Alan Leiner.—1st ed.
[64]p. : ill. ; cm.
Summary : A collection of poems about music.
ISBN 1-56397-178-X
1. Music—Juvenile poetry. 2. Children's poetry. [1. Music—Poetry.
2. Poetry.] I. Strickland, Michael R. II. Leiner, Alan, ill. III. Title.
811.54—dc20   1993
Library of Congress Catalog Card Number 92-81078

Permissions can be found on page 56.

First edition, 1993
Book designed by Charlotte Staub
The text of this book is set in 12-point Post Antiqua.
The illustrations are done in pen and ink.

10 9 8 7 6 5 4

CONTENTS

INTRODUCTION

From the beginnings of language to verse about laser beams, poems and songs have evolved together. There are poems and songs about cowboys, the wilderness, young girls, old men, brick alleys, roaring lions, and the far reaches of outer space. Numerous poets have entitled one of their pieces simply "Song."

Many poets have wanted to capture music's rhythm and rhyme by emphasizing sounds as much as meaning in their word choice and sentence structures. Their intent is to make the reader mentally hear a poem.

Eve Merriam, in her "Advice from a Visiting Poet," said, "Always read a poem twice: once for the words, and once for the music of the words." This is wise advice because poems can sing to you. I urge the reader to use Merriam's suggestion while reading and listening to this anthology. Let the poems sing.

From the high-stepping Russian moujik and the native American rain dance to compact disks, portable stereos, and digital computers, the continuous chord that sounds through this book is musical language.

I have always believed in music as the UNIVERSAL language, cutting across time and distance, generations and cultures. As soon as man could sing and bang a drum, he used songs to facilitate learning, relaxation, inspiration, prayer, and romance. The selections in POEMS THAT SING TO YOU are like a show at a concert hall—they provide visual stimulation to a body of music. Reading fills the mind via the eyes, and a musical poem can be likened to a symphony recorded on paper that can be performed centuries later.

Arnold Adoff spoke of such visual stimulation:

the poem singing into your eyes
it is singing into your eyes
it is the poem into your eyes
it is the poem singing

A poem is meant to be read and reread. POEMS THAT SING TO YOU can be thought of as a soundtrack that can be taken home from a favorite performance to be enjoyed again and again. Then the reader can mix a love for poetry with appreciation of music. Throughout the book drums pound, piano keys are struck, voices rise in song, compact disks whirl, and Mozart even plays rock 'n' roll.

In my adolescent years, I used music for comfort, rebellion, identity, acceptance, and anything else I could stretch its parameters to reach. Music still energizes me like a walk in the sun, and I think of it as a necessity like food, air, and water. Many of us think of music as a special friend.

Music appreciation has been said to be a sixth sense. Fine poetry, like fine music, gives the reader an instant essence of flight, taking him or her far away from the present place and into a myriad of real and imaginary worlds.

Teachers can use POEMS THAT SING TO YOU to encourage a love of poetry in their students with a topic about which young people can't seem to get enough. Students can listen to the music within themselves when they are eager to experience the new and exciting, to harmonize with poems that sing.

Michael R. Strickland

SECTION ONE

Poems That Dance

DANCING IN THE STREET
(As recorded by Martha and the Vandellas)

Calling out around the world are you ready for a brand new beat
Summer's here and the time is right for dancing in the street
They're dancing in Chicago, down in New Orleans, in
    New York City
All we need is music, sweet music, there'll be music everywhere,
There'll be swinging and swaying and records playing and
    dancing in the street.

It doesn't matter what you wear
Just as long as you are there
So come on every guy grab a girl
Everywhere around the world
There'll be dancing, they're dancing in the street.

This is an invitation across the nation, a chance for folks to meet
There'll be laughing, singing, and music swinging, dancing
    in the street

Philadelphia, P.A., Baltimore and D.C., can't forget the Motor
    City now
All we need is music, sweet music, there'll be music everywhere,
There'll be swinging and swaying and records playing and
    dancing in the street.

Oh, it doesn't matter what you wear
Just as long as you are there
So come on every guy grab a girl
Everywhere around the world
They're dancing, they're dancing in the street.

Way down in L.A. everyday, they're dancing in the street
They form a big, strong line, yeah, in time
They're dancing in the street
Across the ocean blue, me and you,
They're dancing in the street.

—William Stevenson, Marvin Gaye, and Ivy Hunter
(Words and Music)

RUSSIAN DANCE

The Russian moujik is mad for music,
For music the moujik is most enthusic.
Whenever an instrument twangs or toots
He tucks his trousers into his boots,
He squats on his heels, but his knees don't crack,
And he kicks like a frenzied jumping jack.
My knees would make this performance tragic,
But his have special moujik magic.

—Ogden Nash

DRY AND PARCHED

Dry and parched
The ground I stand on.
I sing a prayer.
I raise my arms.
I stamp my feet
And move in circles.
Dust rises
And the sun burns
But I keep dancing
And singing.
If I am pure and innocent,
I can call the rain
From the clouds.

—Alonzo Lopez

CELEBRATION

I shall dance tonight.
When the dusk comes crawling,
There will be dancing
    and feasting.
I shall dance with the others
    in circles,
      in leaps,
        in stomps.

Laughter and talk
    will weave into the night,
Among the fires
    of my people.
Games will be played
And I shall be
    a part of it.

—Alonzo Lopez

4

DANCE POEM

come Nataki dance with me
bring your pablum dance with me
pull your plait and whorl around
come Nataki dance with me

won't you Tony dance with me
stop your crying dance with me
feel the rhythm of my arms
don't lets cry now dance with me

Tommy stop your tearing up
don't you hear the music
don't you feel the happy beat
don't bite Tony dance with me
Mommy needs a partner

here comes Karma she will dance
pirouette and bugaloo
short pink dress and dancing shoes
Karma wants to dance with me
don't you Karma don't you

all you children gather round
we will dance and we will whorl
we will dance to our own song
we must spin to our own world
we must spin a soft Black song
all you children gather round
we will dance together

—Nikki Giovanni

THE DANCE

In Breughel's great picture, The Kermess,
the dancers go round, they go round and
around, the squeal and the blare and the
tweedle of bagpipes, a bugle and fiddles
tipping their bellies (round as the thick-
sided glasses whose wash they impound)
their hips and their bellies off balance
to turn them. Kicking and rolling about
the Fair Grounds, swinging their butts, those
shanks must be sound to bear up under such
rollicking measures, prance as they dance
in Breughel's great picture, The Kermess.

—William Carlos Williams

BOOGIE CHANT AND DANCE

Ladies and gentlemen and children, too,
Here are four nice girls gonna boogie for you.
They're gonna turn all around,
They're gonna touch the ground,
They're gonna shake their shoulders
Till the sun goes down.
Hands up! Ha-ha. Ha-ha-ha!
Hands down! Ha-ha. Ha-ha-ha!
Got a penny, call Jack Benny. Ha-ha. Ha-ha-ha!
Got a nickel, buy a pickle. Ha-ha. Ha-ha-ha!
Got a dime, ain't it fine. Ha-ha. Ha-ha-ha!

—Traditional

6

SECTION TWO

Poems That Sound

JUKE BOX LOVE SONG

I could take the Harlem night
and wrap around you,
Take the neon lights and make a crown,
Take the Lenox Avenue buses,
Taxis, subways,
And for your love song tone their rumble down.
Take Harlem's heartbeat,
Make a drumbeat,
Put it on a record, let it whirl,
And while we listen to it play,
Dance with you till day—
Dance with you, my sweet brown Harlem girl.

—Langston Hughes

TUNING UP

I'm at a concert
And the tuba moans.
The tuba moans
And the bassoon groans.
The bassoon groans
And the violin sings.
The violin sings
And the cymbal rings.
The cymbal rings
And the trumpet toots.
The trumpet toots
And the flutist flutes.
The flutist flutes
And the drummer drums.
The drummer drums
And the cello hums. . . .
Then ending all this dissonance
The baton raps and starts to dance.

—Felice Holman

JAZZ FANTASIA

Drum on your drums, batter on your banjos,
sob on the long cool winding saxophones.
Go to it, O jazzmen.

Sling your knuckles on the bottoms of the happy
tin pans, let your trombones ooze, and go husha-
husha-hush with the slippery sand-paper.

Moan like an autumn wind high in the lonesome tree-
tops, moan soft like you wanted somebody terrible,
cry like a racing car slipping away from a motorcycle
cop, bang-bang! you jazzmen, bang altogether drums,
traps, banjos, horns, tin cans—make two people fight
on the top of a stairway and scratch each other's eyes
in a clinch tumbling down the stairs.

Can the rough stuff . . . now a Mississippi steamboat
pushes up the night river with a hoo-hoo-hoo-oo . . .
and the green lanterns calling to the high soft stars
. . . a red moon rides on the humps of the low river
hills . . . go to it, O jazzmen.

—Carl Sandburg

UMBILICAL

You can take away my mother,
you can take away my sister,
but don't take away
my little transistor.

I can do without sunshine,
I can do without Spring,
but I can't do without
my ear to that thing.

I can live without water,
in a hole in the ground,
but I can't live without
that sound that sound that sound that sOWnd.

—Eve Merriam

NEW YEAR'S EVE

Play a thin tune
on a paper horn.
> Old is dying.
> New is born.

Scatter confetti
over the floor.
> Sweep an old year
> Out the door.

Blow up a wish
in a bright balloon.
> Whisper dreams
> To a midnight moon.

Play a loud tune
on a paper horn.
> Old is dying.
> New is born.

—Myra Cohn Livingston

THE TAPE

Poor song,
> going around in your cassette
> over and over again, repeating
> the same old tune,
> can you breathe in there?

Come, song,
> going around in your cassette
> over and over again, break out!
> Let me play you
> fresh on my guitar!

—Myra Cohn Livingston

THE HIGH SCHOOL BAND

On warm days in September the high school band
Is up with the birds and marches along our street,
Boom boom,
to a field where it goes boom boom until eight forty-five
When it marches, as in the old rhyme, back, boom boom,
To its study halls, leaving our street
Empty except for the leaves that descend, to no drum,
And lie still.
In September
A great many high school bands beat a great many drums,
And the silences after their partings are very deep.

—Reed Whittemore

COMPACT DISK

Fast like a frisbee
WHIZZING through the air
my CD is my latest
toy and greatest dance helper.

It could roll down the street
and still play rock.
Mom says I'm too young
to keep the mall in business
so I only have one.

Dancing to my disk
I feel grown up and enlightened,
but when Mom's disk sings Figaro
then I'm frightened
that anyone could like such bizarre noise.

When I get home from school
take out Mom's Mozart
and slide my CD in,
I can almost see
that laser beam spinning hits
just for me, and when the speakers
begin to pound, I feel free.

—Michael R. Strickland

LEWIS HAS A TRUMPET

A trumpet
A trumpet
Lewis has a trumpet
A bright one that's yellow
A loud proud horn.
He blows it in the evening
When the moon is newly rising
He blows it when it's raining
In the cold and misty morn
It honks and it whistles
It roars like a lion
It rumbles like a lion
With a wheezy huffing hum
His parents say it's awful
Oh really simply awful
But
Lewis says he loves it
It's such a handsome trumpet
And when he's through with trumpets
He's going to buy a drum.

—Karla Kuskin

STEEL DRUM

Music always playin'
on my own island.
Reggae, rockers, calypso
the steelband panorama.
Long into the evening
after sun done gone
I keep on hearing the pan man
POM DA DE DE DE DOM POM
sweet on that steel drum!

—Lynn Joseph

AT THE SYMPHONY

The 'cellos, setting forth apart,
Grumbled and sang, and so the day,
From the low beaches of my heart,
Turned in tranquility away.

And over weariness and doubt
Rose up the horns like bellied sails,
Like canvas of the soul flung out
To rising and orchestral gales;

Passed on and left irresolute
The ebony, the silver throat . . .
Low over clarinet and flute
Hung heaven upon a single note.

—Robert Nathan

PLAYER PIANO

My stick fingers click with a snicker
As, chuckling, they knuckle the keys;
Light-footed, my steel feelers flicker
And pluck from the keys melodies.

My paper can caper; abandon
Is broadcast by dint of my din,
And no man or band has a hand in
The tones I turn on from within.

At times I'm a jumble of rumbles,
At others I'm light like the moon,
But never my numb plunker fumbles,
Misstrums me, or tries a new tune.

—John Updike

PIANO

The perfect ice of the thin keys must break
And fingers crash through stillness into sound,
And through the mahogany darkness of the lake
Splinter the muteness where all notes are found.
O white face floating upwards amidst hair!
Sweet hands entangled in the golden snare,
           Escape, escape, escape,
      Or in the coils of joy be drowned.

What is the cabinet that holds such speech
And is obedient to caresses strange
As tides that stroke the long-deserted beach,
And gales that scourge the Peruvian mountain range?
O flesh of wood with flanks aglow with suns,
O quivering as at the burst of monstrous guns,
           Subside, subside, subside,
      Or into dust and atoms change.

Nor can the note-shaped heart, nor can the ear
Withstand your praise, O numbers more appalling
Than ringed and voyaging on the atmosphere
Those heavy flocks of fallen angels falling;
You strike with fists of heaven against the void
Where all but choiring music is destroyed,
           And light, and light, and light,
      Bursts into voice forever calling.

—Karl Shapiro

Poems That Make Melodies

THE POEM SINGING
INTO YOUR EYES

the poem singing into your eyes
it is singing into your eyes
it is the poem into your eyes
it is the poem singing

—Arnold Adoff

ADVICE FROM A VISITING POET

"Always read a poem twice:
once for the words,
and then for the music of the words."

At the public library in New York City
the place for poetry readings
is a room in the basement

where the poet tunes in to the audience
with the subway
an obbligato below

the underground cars race on
to their appointed stations
passengers rush up to the surface

while the words of the poem
move down deeper
into the glowing dark.

—Eve Merriam

ROCK 'N' ROLL BAND

If we were a rock 'n' roll band,
We'd travel all over the land.
We'd play and we'd sing and wear spangly things,
If we were a rock 'n' roll band.

If we were a rock 'n' roll band,
And we were up there on the stand,
The people would hear us and love us and cheer us,
Hurray for that rock 'n' roll band.

If we were a rock 'n' roll band,
Then we'd have a million fans.
We'd giggle and laugh and sign autographs,
If we were a rock 'n' roll band.

If we were a rock 'n' roll band,
The people would all kiss our hands.
We'd be millionaires and have extra long hair,
If we were a rock 'n' roll band.

But we ain't no rock 'n' roll band,
We're just seven kids in the sand
With homemade guitars and pails and jars
And drums of potato chip cans.

Just seven kids in the sand,
Talkin' and wavin' our hands,
And dreamin' and thinkin' oh wouldn't it be grand,
If we were a rock 'n' roll band.

—Shel Silverstein

KIDNAP POEM

ever been kidnapped
by a poet
if i were a poet
i'd kidnap you
put you in my phrases and meter
you to jones beach
or maybe coney island
or maybe just to my house
lyric you in lilacs
dash you in the rain
blend into the beach
to complement my see
play the lyre for you
ode you with my love song
anything to win you
wrap you in the red Black green
show you off to mama
yeah if i were a poet i'd kid
nap you

—Nikki Giovanni

RECORD

I think I know just how the notes should sound,
And yet there's always something in the way
The violins, the horns and woodwinds play
That makes me understand that I have found

A kind of hearing that is strange and new,
A music I have never heard before,
And so I listen   listen more,
asking what it is that Mozart knew

That I must find myself, and hear, although
The next time that I play it, some new phrase
Will whirl within my head for days and days
And come to be a part of all I know.

—Myra Cohn Livingston

WOLFGANG ROCK

If Mozart were alive
He'd be playing lead guitar,
Dancing in the spotlight
And prancing like a star.
His hair would be dyed purple
And his music would be bold.
If Mozart were alive
He'd be playing rock and roll.

—Brod Bagert

FROM **TWO JAZZ POEMS**

yeah here am i
am standing
at the crest of a tallest
hill with a trumpet
in my hand & dark
glasses
on.

bearded & bereted i proudly stand!
    but there are no eyes to see me.
i send down cool sounds!
    but there are no ears to hear me.

—Carl Wendell Hines, Jr.

ON RACHMANINOFF'S BIRTHDAY

Blue windows, blue rooftops
and the blue light of the rain,
these contiguous phrases of Rachmaninoff
pouring into my enormous ears
and the tears falling into my blindness

for without him I do not play,
especially in the afternoon
on the day of his birthday. Good
fortune, you would have been
my teacher and I your only pupil

and I would always play again.
Secrets of Liszt and Scriabin
whispered to me over the keyboard
on unsunny afternoons! and growing
still in my stormy heart.

Only my eyes would be blue as I played
and you rapped my knuckles,
       dearest father of all the Russias,
       placing my fingers
tenderly upon your cold, tired eyes.

                  —Frank O'Hara

A FISH-SCALE SUNRISE

Melodious skeletons, for all of last night's music
Today is today and the dancing is done.

Dew lies on the instruments of straw that you were playing,
The ruts in your empty road are red.

You Jim and you Margaret and you singer of La Paloma,
The cocks are crowing and crowing loud,

And although my mind perceives the force behind the
    moment,
The mind is smaller than the eye.

The sun rises green and blue in the fields and in the
    heavens.
The clouds foretell a swampy rain.

                    —Wallace Stevens

TODAY

Oh! kangaroos, sequins, chocolate sodas!
You really are beautiful! Pearls,
harmonicas, jujubes, aspirins! all
the stuff they've always talked about
still makes a poem a surprise!
These things are with us every day
even on beachheads and biers. They
do have meaning. They're strong as rocks.

                —Frank O'Hara

FROM **THE MAN WITH THE BLUE GUITAR**

I

The man bent over his guitar,
A shearsman of sorts. The day was green.

They said, "You have a blue guitar,
You do not play things as they are."

The man replied, "Things as they are
Are changed upon the blue guitar."

And they said then, "But play, you must,
A tune beyond us, yet ourselves,

A tune upon the blue guitar
Of things exactly as they are."

II

I cannot bring a world quite round,
Although I patch it as I can.

I sing a hero's head, large eye
And bearded bronze, but not a man,

Although I patch him as I can
And reach through him almost to man.

If to serenade almost to man
Is to miss, by that, things as they are,

Say that it is the serenade
Of a man that plays a blue guitar.

—Wallace Stevens

THE PENNY FIDDLE

YESTERDAY I bought a penny fiddle
    And put it to my chin to play,
But I found that the strings were painted,
    So I threw my fiddle away.

If I had but saved up the halfpennies
    That I spent on buns and plums,
A shilling would have bought real music,
    But now the whisper comes.

I shall sell my boots to buy a fiddle,
    And walk about with ankles bare,
I shall laugh in the falling snow-flakes,
    For what should a fiddler care.

—Robert Graves

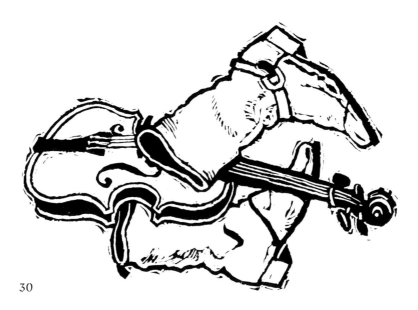

ODE

We are the music-makers,
    And we are the dreamers of dreams
Wandering by lone sea-breakers,
    And sitting by desolate streams;
World-losers and world-forsakers,
    On whom the pale moon gleams:
Yet we are the movers and shakers
    Of the world for ever, it seems.

With wonderful deathless ditties
We build up the world's great cities,
    And out of a fabulous story
    We fashion an empire's glory:
One man with a dream, at pleasure,
    Shall go forth and conquer a crown;
And three with a new song's measure
    Can trample an empire down.

We, in the ages lying,
    In the buried past of the earth,
Built Nineveh with our sighing,
    And Babel itself with our mirth;
And o'erthrew them with prophesying
    To the old of the new world's worth;
For each age is a dream that is dying,
    Or one that is coming to birth.

—Arthur O'Shaughnessy

M., SINGING

Now, innocent, within the deep
Night of all things you turn the key,
Unloosing what we know in sleep.
In your fresh voice they cry aloud
Those beings without heart or name.

Those creatures both corrupt and proud,
Upon the melancholy words
And in the music's subtlety,
Leave the long harvest which they reap
In the sunk land of dust and flame
And move to space beneath our sky.

—Louise Bogan

MY VILLAGE SCHOOL

By a stream
Sits my village school.

By a silver stream
Where chorus of croaking frogs are heard.

The school band
Sits on green grass.

Three instruments
Are all we play.

BOOM BOOM BOOM sounds the bass drum.
RAT-A-TAT-TAT RAT-A-TAT-TAT echoes the snare drum.

The flute, crafted from bamboo,
Sweetly peals DO RE ME.

Barefoot students, dressed in green,
All marching on green grass, sing,

"We're little soldiers marching.
We marched from London to America."

And the chorus of croaking frogs
Mixing in with the chorus of singing children.

My village school brings back
The magic of friends, memory and music.

—Isaac Olaleye

DREAM BOOGIE

Good-morning, daddy!
Ain't you heard
The boogie-woogie rumble
Of a dream deferred?

Listen closely:
You'll hear their feet
Beating out and beating out a—

> YOU THINK
> IT'S A HAPPY BEAT?

Listen to it closely:
Ain't you heard
something underneath
like a—

> WHAT DID I SAY?

Sure,
I'm happy!
Take it away!

> HEY, POP!
> RE-BOP!
> MOP!
>
> Y-E-A-H!

—Langston Hughes

Poems That Sing the Happies and the Blues

PROGRESS

Great-grandpa had a gramophone
That weighed a hundred pounds,

Granddad had a hi-fi
That stood four feet off the ground,

Papa had components
Stacked in stages like a rocket,

And me . . .
I've got a Walkman
I can fit inside my pocket.

—Brod Bagert

A NEW AGE

I asked the old jazzman:
    WHAT INSTRUMENT SHOULD I LEARN TO PLAY?
    THE TROMBONE . . . ?
    OR THE SAXOPHONE . . . ?
    THE LEAD GUITAR OR BASS . . . ?
But the jazzman kinda shook his head,
Then he made a funny face and said:
    CHILD . . . I'M GONNA MAKE YOU WISE,
    YOU YOUNG CATS GOT TO REALIZE
    THAT MUSIC SOUND DONE DIGITIZED
    AND EVERYTHING IS SYNTHESIZED.
    IF YOU WANT TO GET A GIG
    THAT AIN'T GONNA GO AWAY,
    A MULTI-MEDIA COMPUTER
    IS THE INSTRUMENT TO PLAY.

—Brod Bagert

THE MUSICIAN

Maybe you've seen him
Standing there
With his back against the wall
Of a boarded up building.
He's there every day
With that pawnshop violin
Tucked under his chin,
His spiderleg fingers
Dancing hard on the strings
While the other hand
Pumps the bow,
I bet you've seen him there.
He just plays one tune
Over and over
And people never stop.
Even the ones
Who drop in a coin
To clink in his beat-up hat
Turn their heads
When they do it
Like it might embarrass them
to look,
But he doesn't know
Or care about that,
He stands with his eyes closed.
There's only his music,
His one good tune,
For him to be thinking about,
Not a place to stay
Or food or growing old.
His music is a thin blanket

That wraps around him
There in his world
Between his hat and the wall.
He plays his tune
And shuts his eyes
To protect himself from the cold.

—David L. Harrison

PRACTICE

Since Mama bought this stupid horn
I hate the day that I was born
'Cause nothing makes me more forlorn
Than practice practice practice.
Other guys are playing ball
But Mama doesn't care at all,
She's going to drive me up the wall
With practice practice practice.
I deserve to go to jail
For murdering this B-flat scale
And sounding like a dying whale
From practice practice practice.
I tried to tell her I'm not bright
So I could practice half the night
Forever and not get it right,
Why practice practice practice!
But nothing helps, not even tears,
I'm doomed to play this horn for years
With Mama yelling in my ears,
PRACTICE PRACTICE PRACTICE!

—David L. Harrison

THE GLORY OF THE DAY
WAS IN HER FACE

The glory of the day was in her face,
The beauty of the night was in her eyes.
And over all her loveliness, the grace
Of Morning blushing in the early skies.

And in her voice, the calling of the dove;
Like music of a sweet, melodious part.
And in her smile, the breaking light of love;
And all the gentle virtues in her heart.

And now the glorious day, the beauteous night,
The birds that signal to their mates at dawn,
To my dull ears, to my tear-blinded sight
Are one with all the dead, since she is gone.

—James Weldon Johnson

MUSICIAN

Where have these hands been,
By what delayed,
That so long stayed
Apart from the thin

Strings which they now grace
With their lonely skill?
Music and their cool will
At last interlace.

Now with great ease, and slow,
The thumb, the finger, the strong
Delicate hand plucks the long
String it was born to know.

And, under the palm, the string
Sings as it wished to sing.

—Louise Bogan

THE STREET-MUSICIAN

He plays for all the little side-streets, while
A worn, half-wistful smile
Kindles his face when people passing here
Stop and draw near.

So slight a note . . . and yet the thundering town
Has failed to roar it down;
Under the huge despairs, the shattering blows,
It lifts and grows.

Incongruous, unbidden and absurd;
And yet the street is stirred.
As men behold, for all its dark disguise,
The Dream arise!

—Anonymous

PIANO

Softly, in the dusk, a woman is singing to me;
Taking me back down the vista of years, till I see
A child sitting under the piano, in the boom of the tingling
 strings
And pressing the small, poised feet of a mother who smiles
 as she sings.

In spite of myself, the insidious mastery of song
Betrays me back, till the heart of me weeps to belong
To the old Sunday evenings at home, with winter outside
And hymns in the cosy parlour, the tinkling piano our
 guide.

So now it is vain for the singer to burst into clamour
With the great black piano appassionato. The glamour
Of childish days is upon me, my manhood is cast
Down in the flood of remembrance, I weep like a child for
 the past.

         —D.H. Lawrence

Poems That Sing to You

these children singing in stone a
silence of stone these
little children wound with stone
flowers opening for

ever these silently lit
tle children are petals
their song is a flower of
always their flowers

of stone are
silently singing
a song more silent
than silence these always

children forever
singing wreathed with singing
blossoms children of
stone with blossoming

eyes
know if a
lit tle
tree listens

forever to always children singing forever
a song made
of silent as stone silence of
song

—e.e. cummings

46

MY DADDY

my daddy sings the blues
he plays it on his old guitar
my daddy sings the blues
and he plays it on an old guitar
he plucks it on the strings
and he sings about the way things
are

he sings baby, baby, baby
I love you till the day I die
he sings baby, baby, baby
I love you till the day I die
well I hope you love me back
cause you know I don't want to cry

he sings 'Thaniel, 'Thaniel, 'Thaniel
boy I love you deed I do
he sings 'Thaniel, 'Thaniel, 'Thaniel
boy I love you deed I do
well you're a mighty fine fella
and son I'm so proud of you

my daddy sings the blues
he plays it on his old guitar
yeah my daddy sings the blues
and he plays it on that old guitar
he ain't never been on TV
but to me he's a great big star

—Eloise Greenfield

WHEN MAHALIA SINGS

We used to gather at the high window
of the holiness church and, on tip-toe,
look in and laugh at the dresses, too small
on the ladies, and how wretched they all
looked—an old garage for a church, for pews,
old wooden chairs. It seemed a lame excuse
for a church. Not solemn or grand,
with no real robed choir, but a loose jazz band,
or so it sounded to our mocking ears.
So we responded to their hymns with jeers.

Sometimes those holiness people would dance,
and this we knew sprang from deep ignorance
of how to rightly worship God, who after
all was pleased not by such foolish laughter
but by the stiffly still hands in our church

where we saw no one jump or shout or lurch
or weep. We laughed to hear those holiness
rhythms making a church a song fest:
we heard this music as the road to sin,
down which they traveled toward that end.

I, since then, have heard the gospel singing
of one who says I worship with clapping
hands and my whole body, God, whom we must
thank for all this richness raised from dust.
Seeing her high-thrown head reminded
me of those holiness high-spirited,
who like angels, like saints, worshiped as whole
men with rhythm, with dance, with singing soul.
Since then, I've learned of my familiar God—
He finds no worship alien or odd.

—Quandra Prettyman

OLD DEEP SING-SONG

in the old deep sing-song of the sea
in the old going-on of that sing-song
in that old mama-mama-mama going-on
of the nightlong daylong sleepsong
we look on   we listen
we lay by and hear
too many big bells   too many long gongs
too many weepers over a lost gone gold
too many laughs over light green gold
woven and changing in the wash and the heave
moving on the bottoms   winding in the waters
sending themselves with arms and voices
up in the old mama-mama-mama music
up into the whirl of spokes of light

—Carl Sandburg

NATHANIEL'S RAP

It's Nathaniel talking
and Nathaniel's me
I'm talking about
My philosophy
About the things I do
And the people I see
All told in the words
Of Nathaniel B. Free
That's me
And I can rap
I can rap
I can rap, rap, rap
Till your earflaps flap
I can talk that talk
Till you go for a walk
I can run it on down
Till you get out of town
I can rap

I can rap
Rested, dressed and feeling fine
I've got something on my mind
Friends and kin and neighborhood
Listen now and listen good
Nathaniel's talking
Nathaniel B. Free
Talking about
My philosophy
Been thinking all day
I got a lot to say
Gotta run it on down
Nathaniel's way

Okay!
I gotta rap
Gotta rap
Gotta rap, rap, rap
Till your earflaps flap

Gotta talk that talk
Till you go for a walk
Gotta run it on down
Till you get out of town
Gotta rap
Gotta rap
Rested, dressed and feel-
     ing fine
I've got something on
     my mind
Friends and kin and
     neighborhood
Listen now and listen
     good
I'm gonna rap, hey!
Gonna rap, hey!
Gonna rap, hey!
I'm gonna rap!

—Eloise Greenfield

50

ON A BAD SINGER

Swans sing before they die—'twere no bad thing
Should certain persons die before they sing.

—Samuel Taylor Coleridge

THE SINGER

If I had peace to sit and sing,
Then I could make a lovely thing;
But I am stung with goads and whips,
So I build songs like iron ships.

Let it be something for my song,
If it is sometimes swift and strong.

—Anna Wickham

I HEAR AMERICA SINGING

I hear America singing, the varied carols I hear,
Those of mechanics, each one singing his as it should be,
    blithe and strong.
The carpenter singing his as he measures his plank or beam,
The mason singing as he makes ready for work, or leaves
    off work.
The boatman singing what belongs to him in the boat, the
    deckhand singing on the steamboat deck,
The shoemaker singing as he sits on his bench, the hatter
    singing as he stands,
The woodcutter's song, the ploughboy's on his way in the
    morning, or at noon intermission, or at sundown,
The delicious singing of the mother, or of the young wife at
    work, or of the girl singing or washing,
Each singing what belongs to him or her and to none else,
The day that belongs to the day—at night the party of
    young fellows, robust, friendly,
Singing with open mouths their strong, melodious songs.

—Walt Whitman

THE PIPER

Piping down the valleys wild,
    Piping songs of pleasant glee,
On a cloud I saw a child,
    And he laughing said to me:

"Pipe a song about a Lamb!"
    So I piped with merry cheer.
"Piper, pipe that song again;"
    So I piped; he wept to hear.

"Drop thy pipe, thy happy pipe;
    Sing thy songs of happy cheer!"
So I sang the same again,
    While he wept with joy to hear.

"Piper, sit thee down and write
    In a book, that all may read."
So he vanished from my sight;
    And I plucked a hollow reed,

And I made a rural pen,
    And I stained the water clear
And I write my happy songs
    Every child may joy to hear.

— William Blake

NIGHT SONGS

"Pung-la-la," from the frog by my window.
"Shirr-ooo-ooo," from the midnight manicou.
"Ba-lo-ma," from the agouti in the yard.
"Rill-dee-dee," from the mongoose in the tree.
"Gonck-gonck," from the tatou by the pole.
"Urol-el-el," from the matapel.
"Good night," I whisper to my moonlight friends
singing their bedtime songs to the sky.

—Lynn Joseph

SIR DUKE

Music is a world within itself
with a language we all understand,
with an equal opportunity
for all to sing and dance and clap their hands.

But just because a record has a groove
don't make it in the groove,
but you can tell right away at letter "Λ"
when the people start to move.

They can feel it all over.
They can feel it all over, people.

They can feel it all over.
They can feel it all over, people, go!

Music knows it is and always will
be one of the things in life that just won't quit.
But here are some of music's pioneers
that time will not allow us to forget.

For there's Basie, Miller, Satchmo,
and the King of all, Sir Duke
and with a voice like Ella's ringin' out,
there's no way the band can lose.

You can feel it all over.
You can feel it all over, people.

You can feel it all over.
You can feel it all over, people, go!

—Stevie Wonder

PERMISSIONS